This Little Rocket Book

belongs to:

_____

_____

_____

LITTLE ROCKET BOOKS
An imprint of Magi Publications
22 Manchester Street, London W1M 5PG
First published 1998
Text and illustrations © 1998 Little Rocket Books
Text by Linda Jennings
Illustrations by The County Studio
Based on characters and stories by Illtyd Barrie Thomas
Steady Eddie is a registered trademark
of Stobart Management Services
© 1997 Stobart Management Services
Printed by Grafiche AZ, Verona, Italy
ISBN 1 84143 001 3
1 3 5 7 9 10 8 6 4 2

STEADY EDDIE
and his Brilliant Idea

Steady Eddie was driving home, humming happily. The sun was shining and there was a pleasant little breeze. As he drove into a filling station, he said hello to his Scottish friend, Jock the Tartan Tanker. "It's a grand day for a long journey," said Jock, who was driving back up north.

Steady Eddie saw some of his friends, Derek the Digger, Colin the Concrete Mixer and Brian the Brick Wagon, who were helping to build a new supermarket nearby. There was a tipper truck, too, who was in a bit of trouble. He had just driven into a pile of bricks and scattered them everywhere.

Steady Eddie filled up his tank. He called
goodbye to Jock and Derek and the other trucks
who were busy helping Terry the Tipper Truck pick
up all the bricks, then set off home along a country
road. He loved the countryside, even though
nothing exciting ever happened there.
Steady Eddie slowed down when he noticed
a line of cows, walking towards the road.

"LOOK OUT!" he called.
"Don't cross now – it isn't safe!"
"It's all right," they shouted back.
"We have our own crossing place."

To Steady Eddie's surprise, the cows all walked across a bridge, and safely reached the other side. "What a good idea!" he thought. "A little bridge, built specially for the cows."

Although he kept his eyes firmly on the road, Steady
Eddie noticed everyone enjoying the summer
sunshine. Horses were galloping round the fields,
swallows skimmed over the telegraph poles and baby
rabbits played tag in the fields.
But what was that, sitting in the middle of the road?

Steady Eddie quickly checked behind him. Luckily there were no vehicles there. He put on his brakes and stopped. JUST IN TIME! A tiny rabbit crouched, trembling, in front of Steady Eddie's huge wheels.

"What are you doing?" said Steady Eddie. "Did no one tell you how to cross the road safely? I could have knocked you down!"

The little rabbit was too scared to answer him, but a big rabbit hopped over from the bushes. It was his mother.

"I've told him a hundred times to wait for me," she said. "But he's so impatient. He just ran on ahead."

Steady Eddie pulled in at the side of the road,
as Mother Rabbit took her baby to safety.
To Steady Eddie's surprise, a group of small
animals had gathered on the verge.

"It's a terribly dangerous road," said Badger.
"There's nowhere safe to cross at all," said Mouse.
"I have to visit my mother on the other side," said Fox.

"And my babies are so careless, I'm afraid they will be hurt," cried Mother Rabbit.

Steady Eddie felt very sorry
for the animals. He thought
of the cows and their safe crossing
over the road. But you couldn't
build a bridge in such thick woods.
You couldn't have a pedestrian
crossing, either, out here,
deep in the country.
What could you do?

Then, suddenly, Steady Eddie had a BRILLIANT
idea! He would need lots of time and lots of help.
And he wanted it to be a big surprise for the animals.
"Just be patient for a little while," he told them.
"I think I have the answer."

Steady Eddie drove back to the building site where
his friends were still working on the new supermarket.
He explained to them exactly what his plan was, and
at once they all agreed to help.

"We will do it at the end of the day when the road is quiet," said Derek the Digger.
"Can I come along too?" asked Terry the Tipper Truck.
"Of course you can," said Steady Eddie. "We will need all the help we can get."

After returning to the depot to explain what was
happening, Steady Eddie hurried back to wait for his
friends. He put on his hard hat,
all ready for the night's work.
"No time to be lost,"
said Brian the Brick Wagon,
as he offloaded his bricks.
"I'll get a lot done before
sunset," said Derek the Digger,
starting to dig straightaway.

Steady Eddie put up a safety barrier round the worksite.
Some of the animals tried to look over it, but it was
too high.
CRUNCH! CRUNCH! CRUNCH!
BANG! BANG! BANG! went the mysterious
noises behind the barrier.
"What a din!" grumbled Badger.
"If it helps us cross the road in safety, I don't mind,"
said Mother Rabbit.

The trucks worked hard all through the evening. Soon there was a big hole in the ground behind the safety barrier.

"Can you take all this soil?" Derek the Digger asked Terry the Tipper Truck. The truck was very keen to get going. He loaded himself up with soil and began to drive off the site.

Unfortunately, though, he set off too quickly and tipped himself up by mistake.
All the soil fell right back into the hole!
"OH NO!" groaned Derek. "Now we'll have to start all over again!"
"Sorry," muttered Terry. "I was only trying to help."

The animals wondered what on earth was happening. All they could hear were voices from behind the screen.

"You can tip out the concrete mix now, Colin."

"OH NO! NOT THERE!"

"Sorry, I was in too much of a rush," said Colin.

"Never mind, we're nearly ready. Soon be finished!"

Then, just before dawn, as the sun was rising, the noise from behind the safety barrier suddenly stopped. There were no more BANGS and no more CRUNCHES.
Nothing could be heard in the wood, except for the excited chattering of the animals.

"What *was* your brilliant idea, Steady Eddie?" the animals asked. "Can we see what you've done?"
Steady Eddie smiled as the excited animals crept closer to the barrier.
"Close your eyes," he said to them. "And open them when I shout NOW!"

"NOW!" cried Steady Eddie.
The animals all opened their eyes.
"WOW!" cried the squirrels.

"MAGNIFICENT!" shouted Badger.
"UNBELIEVABLE!" squeaked Mouse.
"AT LAST!" said Mother Rabbit, happily.

It was the animals' very own tunnel! It ran right under the road to the other side. No longer would they have to watch for the cars and lorries before they could cross safely.

"THREE CHEERS FOR STEADY EDDIE!" they all shouted as they followed Mother Rabbit and her family through the tunnel to the other side of the road.

"Thank you for all your hard work," Steady Eddie said to his truck friends, as they all made their way home. Back at the depot, he had a nice, long, warm wash to clean off all the dirt from the tunnel-building. "Who says nothing exciting ever happens in the country?" he joked.

I have learned all about road safety. It is very important that you learn all these tips too.

STEADY EDDIE

1   Always **stop**, **look** and **listen** before crossing the road. This means **stop** at the kerb, **look** for vehicles and **listen** for sounds of traffic that you may not be able to see coming. When it is safe, you can step off the kerb and cross the road.

2   You must always **walk**, never run, across a road. If you **run** you are more likely to **fall**.

3   Try to cross a road with a **grown-up** you know. **Hold their hand** while crossing.

4   Always find a **safe place to play**, away from the road.

5   **Never** run straight across a zebra crossing. Sometimes vehicles are going too fast to stop. Always **step carefully** on to the crossing when you are **sure** there is no traffic coming.

6   Never cross the road on a **corner**, the **brow of a hill** or, if you can help it, **between parked cars**. This is because the driver may not be able to see you and you may not see them.

7 Always **wait** at a pedestrian crossing until the **green person** lights up and you have checked

that the **road is clear**. Never cross when the red person is lit up even if you can't see any vehicles approaching.

8   Always wear **bright clothing** to help the drivers see you, especially in winter when it is dark.

9   Never cross a busy main road unless you can cross safely by using a **pedestrian crossing**, a **zebra crossing**, a **footbridge**, a **subway** or at the **traffic lights**. Make sure that you **know where these safe places are** in the area you live.

10   **Keep safe at all times.** Always tell someone where you are going. Never talk to anyone you **don't know.**

Steady Eddie and **RoSPA**
working together to improve road safety awareness.

To make a donation to RoSPA, please write to the Fundraising Manager, The Royal Society for the Prevention of Accidents, Edgbaston Park, 353 Bristol Road, Birmingham B5 7ST

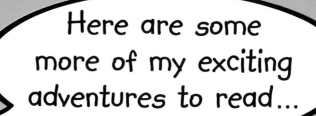

Here are some more of my exciting adventures to read...

STEADY EDDIE FOILS THE PLOT
Steady Eddie is very suspicious when he sees Oliver Overdrive taking computers away from a warehouse. What on earth is he up to? Steady Eddie enlists the help of Bill the Police Car, and the chase is on to retrieve the stolen computers.
ISBN 1 84143 002 1   £2.99

STEADY EDDIE SAVES THE DAY
When Kevin the Coach breaks down on a school trip to France, Steady Eddie is at hand to help all the disappointed children. Will Steady Eddie and the children reach the ferry in time?
ISBN 1 84143 000 5   £2.99

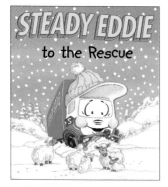

STEADY EDDIE TO THE RESCUE
One winter's day, Steady Eddie is driving carefully along an icy road when he comes across Loretta Lorry who has been battling through the snow to rescue some stranded sheep, and now she is stranded herself! Can Steady Eddie plough his way through the snowy drifts to save the shivering sheep?
ISBN 1 84143 003 X   £2.99

Steady Eddie books are available from most booksellers. In case of difficulty, or if you would like a catalogue of our full range of books, please contact Little Rocket Books, 22 Manchester Street, London W1M 5PG, UK Tel: 0171 486 0925 Fax: 0171 486 0926